I Become
a Delight
to My
Enemies

I Become a Delight to My Enemies

Sara Peters

STRANGE
LIGHT

Library and Archives Canada Cataloguing in Publication data
is available upon request

ISBN: 978-0-7710-7357-1

ebook ISBN: 978-0-7710-7356-4

Book design by Jennifer Griffiths
Cover painting, *Untitled* (2014, 24″ × 36″) by Jessica Mensch
Printed and bound in Canada

Published by Strange Light,
an imprint of Penguin Random House Canada Limited,
a Penguin Random House Company

www.penguinrandomhouse.ca

10 9 8 7 6 5 4 3 2 1

Penguin
Random House
Canada

FOR J

Shame on the flesh that depends on the soul.
Shame on the soul that depends on the flesh.

—GOSPEL OF THOMAS

ASHAMED / VULNERABLE / HIDDEN / DENIGRATED / HURT

+

IRREDEEMABLE / IMPOSSIBLE / FORSAKEN /
HOPELESS / ABANDONED

+

CREATOR / PROGENITOR / RULER / SOWER / SOVEREIGN

+

HOLD / UNDERSTAND / ACCEPT / PROTECT / PRESERVE

+

POWER / CHERISH / EMBODY / INCARNATE / RELEASE

+

THE WAVE / THE EMPIRE / THE FLESH /
THE SPIRIT / THE TOWN

CONTENTS

We poured them in. We poured all of our voices into a single black box. Could we have been anyone? Could this have been anywhere?

A CHORUS OF GHOSTS

After the Town was formed on top of an underground
lake, after the northeast cliff became the site of our disembodied, polyphonic singing, after the Chancellor
purchased the Farmhouse, after the neighbouring island
was established as a burial ground for our tender and
hapless mayors, and after the Oracle assumed her
stance, there was a list of questions about the Town that
we took it upon ourselves to answer.

Why did this Town exist/
Where was it in time and space/
By what rules was it governed/
How did the Chancellor come to power/
What happened at his Farmhouse/
Why this need for subjugation/
What caused the Town's collapse/

Ships still arrive at the docks and unload berries and
seeds; surveyors tramp over the hills and knot orange
tape around trees; the air shimmers with violet electricity
and abandoned wifi networks:

atownlikeanyother
thistownlikenoother
getyourownfuckingwifi
icantstandmyselfwhenyoutouchme
13inchesssss
gnosticcontacthigh
ibecomeadelighttomyenemies

In a cluster of bluish shadows we stretch our legs and crack our necks, then we run like water through pine needles. Our thousands of eyes light on nothing that has not been ravaged. We could retreat into a collective vacancy. We could avoid coming into colour and sound.

Terror had formed us and power had held us in place, but we were prepared to relinquish our secrets and pass into allegory. In this record of the Town's stories, you will feel our presence: the voice beneath each voice. Let us remain unseen. But let us be missed.

FLIGHT RECORDER

We were born
            knowing nothing of our bodies except

that we needed to discard them

and after years of subjecting these bodies

to reckless gymnastics, frequent,
            deliberately contracted illnesses,
                        general lack of plenitude,
and nonspecific sorrow,

at last it was our turn to rappel down the cliff.

Rope shot through our hands.
Something burned behind us—not the Town—
and we were weary,
            bent necks topped with withered faces,
            our flesh in ghastly shambles.

Some of us were so empty we billowed,
some of us had shoulders

                        rubbed to nearly nothing
            by the backpacks we carried.

Who had seen us before?
Various tellers, conductors, and bakers.
The Chancellor.
The moths in our clothes, the mice in our walls.

We peeled our dinner from the rocks at the shore,
              we were prepared to stay, we'd wait.

French-braided Elizabeth, naked beneath a mohair blanket,
the cousin, in flip-flops and gold splash pants
(a modest person,
              whose only goal was to have sex with God)—

Once I was faultlessly beautiful, and my life depended upon it. I groomed my trembling, long-legged animal. I felt great love, I felt great fear: either way, to you, it hardly mattered.

under the slight, wet wind we tended first to our fires,
then only to our breathing,
as we marked the arrival
of nothing and no one.

That night, we all lay in the tent,
watching the bodies of insects
              in shadow cross over its skin,
until we all dropped into

the same sickened dream.
For all this time we'd thought the sensation of living
              was a hand at our throat in a grip
that was ours to loosen, once we reached the shore—

for all these years we'd held the belief
that we'd been designed for this journey,

that we were worth being greeted at the end of it
by faceless beings who would approach from all sides,
         pull the pins from our limbs and our hair,

and lay upon us,

        with nearly

unbearable tenderness,

             dozens of hands—

Harriet was given no love of any kind, for the Townspeople wanted a mystic, and they thought they could create one through torture. They believed that a mystic would bring spiritual complexity to their Town— the same thinking that often leads rich people to take up Buddhism in later life. The Townspeople chose Harriet, and then subtracted shelter and affection. Education had never been part of the question, and sex, they imagined, would take care of itself. She was kept in a stable, fed raw flour and fallen fruit and made to drink water from a hose. Her desire to make jokes at her own expense was crushed, for it was a suspect quality, in such a young person. And then, one April, Harriet was let loose unsupervised in a field.

She parcelled out her time building homes for herself under trees—this life was not that different from the life that was normally hers. Burrowing moles left behind small packets of grass, which she collected and formed into beds for the animals she thought might approach. Meanwhile, the Townspeople produced a yellowish, oniony sweat, their eyes bulged with concentration,

as they worked day and night to not love her.
Individual successes were rewarded: who
could see, in a telescope as in a dream, the
girl shivering as she slept beneath bark, and
refrain from wincing? Who could bear to
watch her try to remove her lips and eye-
lashes, which she had been told were purely
decorative, and not interfere?

A river ran by Harriet's field. Once she saw a
child, attended by two women in halter tops
that featured reindeer kicking up showers
of sequin snowflakes. The women held the
child up by her armpits and skimmed her
feet across the surface of the water, barely
wetting her soles. *Where are your clothes?*
the child said to Harriet, having spotted
her. The women stopped their movements:
Who? That night, Harriet built a bed for
this child, too. Later that week, animals
finally approached—the thin wolves, the
spring bears—but they did not sniff Harriet
lightly and then, overwhelmed by her innocence and purity of heart, depart. The
Townspeople watched the encounter in their
telescopes; they could not reach her slowly
enough. They wove toward her with wonder
and delight, as if moving through close-set
trees toward a sudden, sourceless waterfall.

—

Harriet was later sealed like a gumball in a clear plastic globe and suspended over the Town square, while everyone waited to see if the skin grafts would take hold. The skin of her thighs became the skin of her cheeks, the skin of her back newly coated her front. Strangely, she indeed became a mystic, but not the right type, for her sense of humour bubbled back up, and her attempts to traverse between spiritual planes typically ended in broken hands and feet, and evermore-delicate surgeries. Harriet went about her calling with a steady cheer that the Townspeople found both admirable and appalling. She would rise in the morning and not even take coffee before flinging herself over and over again at the spiked and burning veil between the worlds.

My face in the dirt. Crushed to violets and lemony grass. With shut eyes I see—

Once while walking the dirt road I grew up on I met an old man
Whom I did not recognize as the Chancellor so when he said *help help*
My leg I bent and peered into his wound
And saw that it contained my whole world in miniature:
My misplaced hair dryer, the fish sticks and ketchup
Of my childhood, the wood I'd split the week before—
All that circled me, all that plagued me, all that formed me, held in
his wound—
And that wound was swollen and hot with infection so I said *let me help*
And it was then that he stuffed his dick down my throat
Leaving no room for anything else including my soul or his

And when he came he vanished and I was left lying on the dirt road feeling
Not terror or pain but ecstatic recognition—
I recognized everything around me: the ugly speech of the frozen river
The frogs in the ditches, the roots of the spongy moss,
I saw the foundation of the Farmhouse, I saw the buried women—

You know that feeling when the fabric between your dreaming
And your waking life is thinning is thinning so desperately fast
And you cannot help but cling to it
And in your crude clinging cause it to further dissolve?
You know that feeling in a dream when you're seconds away from orgasm
Or flying or finally being able to haul yourself out of the sucking mud
and run?
It was as if I had finally been granted permission
To re-enter and complete that unfinished and longed-for dream—

HOOVES

She left me,
      walking away through fields of carrots and corn.
I recalled every time

I had embarrassed myself in her presence,
        been dirty, sick, stupid, and drunk,
and I wanted to reel all those memories back into myself,
    though I knew they would corrode me,
        for I was not like her,
with a mind like a typesetter's drawer.

At first the Townspeople brought offerings,
    sugary wine and chocolates in obscure flavours:
fire, copper, pavement-after-summer-rain.

They brought these things because they were desperate,
for I was the only doctor, though I had none of the qualities
    you might expect:
      clear eyes, strong hands,
        an abstract commitment to humanity.

For days after she left me, I persevered,
      threw out my old bras,
      neatened my eyebrows,
      pierced my ears,
      streaked my nails gold,
      but I was too frightened

to open my door.
Townspeople gathered outside my windows,
          five deep at each pane, thinner every day,
their jewellery tarnishing. Meanwhile

ferns refurled, light snow whirled down, and I could hear
          the soft wood of my house
          giving way. At every turn

I felt my brain's black rot slosh in my skull.
          I woke to the sound of some foreign sea in my ear.

And so I ran.
At first I took the path she'd walked to leave me.
I ran into new seasons, new ages.
I ran till my hooves wore down completely,
          then I wobbled on stumps.

The Townspeople and their ailments,
          their cancers and pregnancies, nearly forgotten.

My loyalty only to myself, even though
I'd discarded my name.

I staggered on my kneecaps, I had grown very thin, and yet

if I balanced at a certain angle,
          my features were not unbeautiful to me.

I moved through old lands, old industries.
What was left of my legs
        contained much impacted material: gravel and dirt,
            but also cigarette butts, takeout spoons,
                pennies and french fries and dimes
                    all driven up into the flesh,

but the real humour came
when I wore myself down to my pelvis.

        I laughed as I rolled forth,
        but not the laughter you're imagining:
        black, deranged, torn; it was the laughter

of a good-natured person
who has jogged into a telephone pole.

I gave myself over to feats of concentration:

how long could I live with this stick in my eye,
with my neck at this angle?
I had always been clean, and luckily in the later months

the rain kept me in the manner
to which I was accustomed.
And then, one hour, I was subjected to a vision.

At this point summer was collapsing into fall
        and I had worn myself down to my rib cage,
            yet still I rolled forth.

In this vision my body had been refurbished,
and I walked to a field of bluebells and stood just at the edge,
for I could no more imagine trampling the flowers
than I could imagine trampling
a field of human faces.

I stood just at the edge of this field, and Townspeople
appeared in a circle around it,
each one healthy and well tended, as if, in my absence,
they had taken their bodies into their own hands.

I felt a luxurious contentment in this, as we all drew closer,
this makeshift community, and noticed
the banked glow of our skins.

But I was torn early from this vision,
before it could bring me true comfort or clarity.

I woke alone at the end of a stranger's driveway,
having worn myself down
                                        to my broad shoulders,
which during the course of my journey I had come to love,
if only because

they resembled hers, which I remembered in detail:

specifically how they looked in her sweater,
as she walked away.

Beneath my house the seasons moved in waves. I despised the rank, custardy sunlight. The arrogant needlework of winter.

THE CORNER STORE CLERK VOICES
HIS OPINION

Some Saturdays it's one after another, sodden or rain-streaked, even on dry nights, transparent umbrellas, makeup melting off, wearing "shirts" that are really just complex and colourful bras, buying their sour gummy worms then whispering to me, asking to hide in the storage room, or just behind the counter, just for a moment, just until X stops following them, using their eyes, *brandishing* their eyes, using their hair, *wielding* their hair, their hair the colour of persimmons or lavender flowers, but I am no fool, I don't offer protection, I tell them, safety starts with *you.*

THE SIX-FINGERED WOMAN

On a midday soaring into the nineties
the six-fingered woman came down from her home
in the big dry hills where few people lived.

She came down at the family's invitation,
which had been issued breathlessly
in the moments after their nine-year-old son's
near drowning.
      No one had thought she'd take them up on it.
      But here she was,

walking the gravel drive,
      with her yellowed blouse and peculiar gait.
      Her white hair rose and tangled in the breeze,
she carried a knit knapsack and wore rubber shoes.

         For a few moments before ringing the doorbell
she lingered in the garden, moving among
stone Buddhas, frogs and faeries, touching the flowers,
      as if it were her right.
      (The parents twitched the curtain closed.)
      Minutes later

she was in their house, fingering wedding photos,
showing weird interest in the pepper grinder.
Even the older sister came down to look—
the older sister who had lately retreated so far into herself

it was doubtful she'd ever emerge.
The six-fingered woman removed
        her rubber shoes as she talked,
       and the parents gagged:

she was also six-toed. The father,
who had always prided himself on his ability to
make women laugh,
was silent.

      The six-fingered woman was a piano teacher,
a swimmer, a pragmatist, though she admitted
     to visiting Mystic Rosa once a month.

How had she even reached the son in time,
      when she had been sitting with her fizzy water
      and polka dots,
              many metres from the waves,
watching an empty canoe
          break apart on the rocks?

The parents had to admit
     that the six-fingered woman moved
with indisputable grace and dexterity,

and also she had brought a tin of lemon cookies.
But she seemed not to realize that the cookies
         were furred with blue mould;
        she ate them anyway,
and asked the son to play the piano. The son remembered

that after he'd slipped off the rock,
　　　　and after his annoyance with the grasping waves
　　　　had flashed in four seconds
　　　　into a terror that burned new channels in his brain,

the six-fingered woman was there
　　　　pulling him up, her hair streaming
around the new planet of her underwater face.

For days after he had only to shut his eyes
　　　　　　to conjure the feeling of being gathered
　　　　　　　not just into arms,

but into a warm white radiance,
　　　　into strength without effort or end, strength
　　　　　　　　to be deployed forever

　　　　　　only on his behalf,
in the service of understanding, protecting, and loving him.

At least, that had been his impression.

But now he was bound

not to the face and body of a saviour-seen-through-water,
but to an old woman plopping beside him on the bench,

dropping crumbs on the keys

　　　　　　crying for no discernible reason

You're young
but I ask you
to wait until
no one
recognizes
your slang.
Your music
and food. I am
old; no one
knows I am
modern to a
fault.

MY SON COMES HOME WITH HIS WOMEN

I am full of dread when my son visits with his fleet of women.

To clarify: when he comes home it is only ever with one woman, but I see all his discards following her like ghosts.

They are always beautiful, these women, and educated, far more educated than my son.

He steers them through Town with his hand at the base of their spine.

The last one had hair that shot down her back like a water-fall and the next will have hair that shoots down her back at the speed of light.

Their eyes are uniformly kind, and their trappings of skin look lit from within—my son would never select a woman without a radioactive glow.

They wear mountain-climbing clothes when my son wants them to demonstrate their athleticism and lack of female vanity, and they wear tight lace dresses with rectangular cut-outs and long zippers when my son wants them to look pretty.

Accordingly, their bodies are called either *lean* or *slender*.

Regardless, they cram my son into their mouths as instructed.

They retreat to their bedrooms for nearly the whole visit.

Sometimes they huddle under fleece sheets, sweating out flus.

They accept cups of hot water and lemon, they roll their eyes at their own silliness if they are observed pulling stuffed animals from their luggage.

They speak tenderly of my son's social ease, his love of travel, his friendliness with strangers.

His willingness to talk to *anyone*.

He's such a goofball, they say.

He has so much potential.

It's true: my son brims with verve and pep.

He loves babies and small children; he drinks pints of blended kale and ginger.

His youthful acne's vanished.

He strides through my house examining objects, often breaking them, and then placing them down again, in different rooms.

You see, I manage—without effort, or intention—to provoke violent feelings in men. Over and over again. You might think it was deliberate; you might think I was determined.

I didn't mind when the Chancellor's people came
When they found me still lying on my dirt road
When they produced a suitcase
When they folded my body into a painful square
So that it might fit inside

I didn't mind
Being pulled along the dusty road for hours with only two open inches
of zipper
To breathe through

One moment I saw the orange and pink remains of the sun over water
The next I saw stars

Now it's a November morning and I'm holed up in the Farmhouse
As I have been for six months
I'm playing a game of pulling my turtleneck over my head
Entirely covering my face
And then drinking coffee through the fabric
Because it doesn't work, because it burns and dirties me, it satisfies like
little else

I have not lived variously enough to have my own story, so instead I will tell the story of my mother figure. We live on a boat called the *Forty Foot*, and on it I have grown from infancy to childhood to adolescence. The *Forty Foot* is orange and below deck is a propane stove where we boil water for hot chocolate. There's a pump-to-flush toilet. The windows are round or diamond-shaped. The blankets are plaid wool, and the pillows are plastic sacks stuffed with feathers. Our Town in the distance rhythmically blackens then glows. Sometimes there are other boats, heavier with beer than people, far off though borne by the same waves.

I do not know how my mother figure produces fresh water or where she finds the potatoes and cherries and spinach that keep me energetic, that keep my muscles long and firm. Or how we prevent the boat from capsizing, or how often and where we dock, or how far away the Town really is, brightening, darkening, most visible during our nightly aerobics.

Late in life, my mother figure found me, a baby in a trash compactor. She had started living as a man when she entered the monastery: with bound breasts and loose robes she nearly passed, and the gentle indifference of her brothers made up the deficit. The monks went on supply runs (flour, salt, sugar, and matches), and frequently stopped for hamburgers while travelling home. This was when she found me, and discarded her old life in the same second she discarded her milkshake. She tells me that my life is the life she once craved.

Her early years are a mystery to me. I know at eight she ran from her home when her mother didn't believe what was happening. Even though in words and gestures and drawings, in bedwetting, in nightmares, she told her. I understood, for in my own early years, I too could barely believe in my mother figure's former life. How had it actually happened? It made me feel boring. It made me feel naive. She spoke, and I felt stupid. How did I know enough of the world to feel stupid? How did I know enough of the world to feel boring? But this is her story, not mine. I have not lived variously enough to have my own story.

I want to tell you how it feels to have only lived one way. To have only spoken to one person. Even I know that my true spirit is empty. Even I know that my true soul is barren. My mother figure tells me I have not developed empathy. And I've prodded my heart and found it cold; I've caught my own eye and hurled it back.

I understand that as humans grow they experience cycles of pain and disorder, they love and lose each other, they are exalted and cherished and then shamed and broken, and out of these cycles they form their stories and, in turn, their natures. But I have no stories of my own, for my every moment has been observed, and nothing has ever belonged solely to me. Some days I talk to the fish until my mouth goes dry. I have spent so long examining my face that its actual features are a mystery to me.

I fill myself with the stories of my mother figure, for it lends shading and resonance to my life, and it brings her peace. Sometimes, in thinking through these stories, I substitute my name for hers. She has told me that this empathy exercise could be dangerous, but still she has given consent and encouragement. She wants her stories to become mine, too, so the burden is divided and she is freed, slightly, from her captivity. I submit to my mother figure's various waves. There is no retreat from her water and light. I want to produce human feeling within myself; I want to coax my own nature to fruition, for every plant I've tended and every creature I've netted died in its youth. And, despite the data of my life, I know nothing of the bottom of the sea, except that it's also called cruel.

As a child, I was made to feel extraordinarily grateful for my own suffering. At the time I had no idea who or what I was becoming, just that it was other. How quickly I became what they despised.

Our teacher wobbles into the room on heels, trailing bandages. Her pants are so tight we can see the outline of her vulva. Our teacher is over-prepared. But her PowerPoint slides are no match for our scorn. She thinks that she is the most educated person in the Town but we are about to show her that she is the base bottom. We will not rest until our teacher has been jabbed from every angle. Look at how she illustrates her slides with pencils and apples and cheerful young blonde people gnawing both. Listen to her ankles crack as she scurries across the floor, keeping her eyes on her toes. Is she old enough to have sore hips? Ten minutes in she guiltily remembers to throw back her shoulders and straighten her spine. By twenty she pulls her nose every minute or two, and it reddens and drips.

Our teacher's heels are as high as icicles. None of us is listening to her lecture on dental health, on how lemon acid can ruin even the snowiest, hardiest teeth. Instead of watching the YouTube tutorial on flossing, we watch our teacher aging and wrinkling before us, covering her own bad teeth with her big, coarse hands. Our teacher's hair is cut into an imprecise bob, and though she tries to tame it with coconut oil (we have investigated her purse), still it sticks up in the back, the only part of her that one could call defiant. Our teacher is allergic to chalk but she was too shy to request a whiteboard, so she scrawls on the blackboard and sneezes into her elbow. Thirty minutes into the class it is break time thank god, for our teacher's pants have ridden further up her crotch and the camel toe is, we all decide, pretty intense. *Pussy,* we hiss, when she turns her back.

We wish to control our teacher's body. We wish to tell her which expressions do not suit her face, which clothes do not suit her figure. What can you do with a face so desperately naked as the face of our teacher? What can you do with a teacher moving toward you, arms outstretched, chest filleted open and heart pulsing publicly in its ghastly nest, forty feet of intestines spilling behind her like a bridal train? Why has our teacher not learned to tuck back into herself everything of fragility or value? Her face is so painfully open, the protective foil peeled back and thrown away. When will she learn that there's no scrap of earth we don't populate? How can we teach her to thrive in this world that we govern?

I thought myself unique in my frenzied maintenance of my hair and face and body. I secretly believed that no one tried as hard as I did, that no one was so seamlessly man-made. That no one knew how desperate I was.

I was once a woman who drank with men
(Many women drink with men)
Their ghosts roam fitfully afterwards

Or else they're found by the Chancellor and taken here, to the Farmhouse
This is the birth of tragedy,
Of absolute chaos, total darkness, and complete disaster
This is the invention of processed meat
I will myself someday
Be processed meat; I eat too poorly to be fit for anything else
Protein bars and very little water, toast with the bad kind of peanut butter

Our fridge is stacked with placentas in vacuum-sealed bags
I travel painfully up and down the worn black stairs; we all do
We want a chorus;
We crave a refrain

Outside it's late fall:
Wet ground, folded grass, wormy apples
For fun I stand in front of a projection of waves crashing over and over
We carve salad bowls out of fallen oaks and sell them at the farmer's
market in Town
In the morning we line up for the bathroom, silent and morose, some
of us struggling
With hangovers made so much worse by our pregnancies

The Chancellor claims that the dogs will hurl themselves
Through the bay windows
To protect us

I remember when my daughter began to hate men. The river outside of the room she slept in was now choked with them; they floated downstream without struggling, their football jerseys or suits and ties or loose yoga clothing partly torn off and trailing behind them. Demolished, crushed, vanishing men.

My daughter had been supplied, early in her life, with a narrow white cat that appeared nightly like an icicle in her doorframe, guarding her room, and this cat appeared to hate men, too, though it was itself technically male. It hissed and spat when my husband or any of his brothers or friends entered my daughter's room.

The first time I noticed my daughter actively hating men she was six, and we were in a grocery store. It is important to know that earlier in the day a customer had smashed a bottle of rosemary and peppermint shampoo. A young man, a teenager, walked by wheeling a cart full of radishes. His blockish white smock and blockish white shoes appeared to have been constructed from the same material, and the front of his smock was stained with what must have been animal blood, though my daughter openly speculated.

Passing by us the young man bared his teeth at my daughter in a lascivious way seconds before stepping on the shampoo puddle, slipping backwards and cracking his head on the concrete floor, his teeth vanishing back into his mouth and the cart tipping on top of him, hundreds of radishes rolling out and gradually covering his fallen body like petals.

The second time that my daughter's true and everlasting hatred of men surfaced was at the Town's museum, when she saw a painting of Penthesilea, the Amazon queen, disembowelling one of Odysseus's men. My daughter, nine by now, started clapping when she glimpsed it from sixty feet, and clapped louder and faster, the closer we got.

There were multiple instances of open man-hating during my daughter's teenage years, but the one I recall with the greatest clarity happened in early fall after she had been taken by a friend to a lavender field that they had planned to pillage to stuff pillowettes. This friend, female of course, was treacherous: she outwardly sympathized with my daughter's man-hating ways, while plotting against her in secret. They roamed the field for fewer than fifteen minutes before men began to pop out from behind trees—members of her co-ed volleyball team, the treacherous friend told my daughter.

Later, my daughter decided she didn't want to attend college, but when subjected to an avalanche of criticism (mostly, I am sad to say, from me) she relented, and chose a school that admitted only women. Being my man-hating daughter she lasted one semester only and appeared home in December to tell me that there had been a mixer with the "sibling college" several miles down the road. My daughter claimed to have miniaturized several hundred men from this mixer and smuggled them home in a jumbo bottle of Robaxacet. She did this, she told me, in order to observe their behaviour under stress.

I avoided checking in on the laboratory that her room gradually became. I suppose I did not understand the extent of her power—which would not, in any case, have been a power I knew, a power I recognized, a power that came from this Town. And I can only assume that those experimented-upon men are the same men currently clogging our river; that once my daughter has completed her tests she crushes them quietly, returns them to size, and places them (perhaps with unaccountable tenderness?) in the water, so that they may pass quietly to some other side, arms crossed, like many hundreds of Ladies of Shalott.

But what she saw never frightened her. Outside: deer tiptoed over the lawn. Inside: a hollow plastic octopus she slowly filled with sand.

I KNOW YOU ARE YOU, AND REAL

One year after my sister is dragged to the Farmhouse
I place an ad in the newspaper that says Let's Go Swimming

The woman I later meet at the edge of the lake is perhaps
    three times my age and so thin
I laugh as I imagine her scanty dinners
A bowl of brown rice
A single steamed green vegetable
The simmered stem of some ascetic flower

She is disgusted by my smoking
My matted hair
She snatches the cigarette out of my mouth and slaps me
    across the face and my tears
Which have been so long absent
Are suddenly there and my vision is bright and clean

Beside us
The lake steams
Apple cores and beer cans float around its rim

She strips to boxers and then she takes off my clothes too
The trees are so thickly green
I don't worry about my nudity—the Town is a mile away
And I know I'll seem to be part of the greater landscape
As in a bad painting

When she kneels and starts working on my shoes
I close my eyes and place my hand upon her head

I want to test the water with a finger or foot but watching
    her dive
Makes me ashamed of my hesitancy
So I climb an overhanging tree
And sit for a moment in the fragrant creaking alien arms

And then I drop into the lake from that height
Not knowing if there will be rocks below

In the moments before I hit the water
I love her more than I've ever loved anyone

The lake is so silty and fetid
It feels like when I was a child
And forced to use my sister's old bathwater
After she had been lifted out and towelled dry

Now
What wouldn't I give to swim in my sister's dirt?
There is nothing
There's nothing I would not give

How could our parents have thought that water fit for
    another person
After they had washed her thin oily hair in it
After they'd cleaned the dirt from her toes

This water is as warm as saliva and the bottom is covered in
    strange lumps
My companion is miles ahead already
A muddy blur
I want to ingratiate myself to her

I want to receive the full measure of her attention
Without doing anything to provoke it
And certainly without revealing
That her attention matters to me in any way

In other words
I am ordinary

I want to tell her
I know how to suffer
With my swallowing and my injecting
With my snowbanks and my hangovers
With the terror that turns
My organs black and sour

She insists we follow the river that feeds the lake
We swim against a ruthless current until we can go no further
Until we are swept back cursing

Still she says nothing
Still I learn nothing
I await what I know will never arrive
I await what I wouldn't recognize if it did
(My suffering acquires a mock-spiritual cast)

We reach the bank
I want to thank her then break her
Gently apart at the joints like a chicken
But there on the bank in front of my eyes
She dissolves like sugar whisked into water

I emerge from the lake less clean than when I entered
Our Town's nightwatchman circles the water
Even though it is nowhere near evening
He wears huge black goggles and reinforced rubber boots
He taps his way forward with the aid of a walking stick

I lie back in my round iridescent-pink sunglasses
I think pink is the most influential colour in the world

People motor by in a boat
They're laughing and passing around a baby
I feel my usual revulsion at laughter and babies and groups

I look into the opal on my finger and if I unfocus my eyes
I can see my sister swimming inside the fiery lake at its core

Lately I cannot decide
What I believe

Do I believe in release
Do I deserve release
Will I be released

In a very short time, I lost everything. The way forward is hidden from me, as is the way back. And I cannot remain here, of course.

Birds pass overhead, knowing the air currents so well
They barely tilt their leathery wings

Each afternoon, up the dirt driveway, which is several miles long and
switchbacked,
Rolls a white SUV, one of the driverless ones
I'm usually hidden behind barely enough of a hill
I let my fingers drift lazily through my hair until they end up in my mouth
How many vegetarians still standing? the Chancellor says when he emerges
And sets out our platters of factory meats

I say to my mind, stumble around you filthy mess but don't you ever
leave me
I say to my heart, what will I do with this poor abject heart now?
I screamed for the mayor,
I screamed for the state,
I hacked my way to the bleeding edge of my brain

THE DERMATOLOGIST AT THE FARMER'S MARKET

The dermatologist had, at some point, flirted with everyone's daughter. He had countless sensitive, spindly children—he was what you might call a hoarder. Each child had an unusually flexible body and an operatic emotional range. The dermatologist would walk the Town's main street in wraparound eclipse glasses and a black wool suit that overspilled at the collar and cuffs with the froth of his white shirt. Mothers would duck into the credit union or the Triangle Pub when they heard him coming. The dermatologist lived with his children and his wife in a split-level bungalow that he nonetheless called Spruce Acres.

The thing about him was, his wife kept having babies. Once a year, someone would spot her at the evening farmer's market, buying crocheted Celtic cross tea cozies, and you'd have to look carefully but there was nearly always a baby somewhere on her person. She would duck and weave when you spoke to her but eventually she would lift the corner of her coat and you would see the new child. Or was it the old one? Your eyes would move from her feet, which were always slippered, to her hair, which had gone from grey to white. The vendors would cast their eyes down and search for nothing in their tills until she passed. Sometimes she'd finger a beach glass necklace, or a jar of blackberry jelly. The dermatologist, picking up the rear, would pause at the SPCA cage, take off his gloves, and stick his fat, clean fingers through the bars for the kittens to lick. Their children, meanwhile, would have scattered like roaches to enter the limbo contest.

Above this scene, the moon scuttles into place like a sil-

verfish. The evening farmer's market features a bagpiper,

who is at this moment warming up in the corner, at

tooth-loosening decibels. No one can hear what anyone is

saying, least of all what the dermatologist is saying to his

I remember
this Town's
early years,
before I met
the derma-
tologist.
Everyone was
so tall, so
ornately
robed, their
braids full of
jewels and laid
carefully down
their backs.
Meanwhile, I
never had a
single opinion
worth
defending.

wife, as he leans over and tugs back her shawl (beneath

which there had been some slight movements, earlier in the

day, movements that have since ceased).

What is the point of this report? Is it the predatory

nature of the dermatologist, the subservience of his wife,

the complacency of the Town, the eyes of the hoarded

children? Which child will be the first to challenge the der-

matologist's dominion? Or will they remain loyal to the

universe of his making? Either way, they are lucky to be

so young and flexible. Look at how deep their backs bend

as they travel under the metre stick.

CHAPTER 1

[. . .] Suddenly, our mother found herself pregnant with twins. It was as if we had plummeted down into her body from an astral height. [. . .] She was only eleven, and she'd not imagined that her brother's activities could produce even one such result, let alone two. [. . .]

CHAPTER 2

After our births, she retreated from the social life of the Town, but her real sadness began once Mirjana and I walked and talked. How often she shaved our heads, how frequently, how publicly, she exfoliated our flesh, standing in the front yard in a flurry of flakes. The homemade bleach-based lotions she applied to our faces, how she filed our fingers down to nubs. [. . .] Eventually, everyone knew, there would be nothing left of us but a pile of skin clippings.

CHAPTER 3

So at six we were taken to the Farmhouse orphanage, to grow into our twisted forms [. . .], and my sister and I were bound not only to each other but also to a suite of arcane laws. These laws were set by our minders (a rotating cast of Townspeople, overseen by the Chancellor), and written every morning in magic marker on the kitchen white-board. They varied from the officious, to the practical, to the inexplicable, to the comedic. One morning the law would inform us that we needed to braid our hair together, so we staggered around attached at the head. Another evening the law would be that we must make warthog noises when we ate the carrots at dinner. [. . .] For several years, the law was that we were never to read books about people, only animals, which we were told we more closely resembled. Big Ben, Black Beauty, Old Yeller. Of course, these books featured families as well, since the stories hinged on how human-like the animals became, but we were told to ignore these deviant elements.

CHAPTER 4

Mainly, we were kept separate from the other children, but once a dusty child snuck into our room at night. Mirjana was asleep, and I had just finished spraying foam into my hair and rubbing my arms with glitter cream. [. . .] I stood with my back to the bureau, and the child stood in front of me and we looked at each other, and then she reached across and viciously pinched my arm.

Immediately, I recognized her. Immediately, I loved her. I loved her anger, of course, which resembled mine, but I also loved that she wanted so badly to have an effect on me. I knew it was important to accept the pinching as part of my fate. Tears pooled in my eyes and ran down my face, but my voice remained steady as I recited to her an old poem about pine trees, and the ghosts snagged on their needles. The child was perhaps four years old, and her cloudy eyes betrayed fear and a complete lack of understanding. But I knew her. And she knew me. She, too, was a gnostic.

CHAPTER 5

Each day, we would set out striving to forget the previous one. Each night, a minder would bring us a pill the size and colour of a cherry, and after swallowing one, darkness would drop over our heads like a photographer's cloth. Each morning, the sun set its burning face at our bars. We were guarded by a dog with a face like coughed-up meat. [. . .] And yet, once I could think, I thought: This life is manageable.

CHAPTER 6

We had been told that reactions to us, should we creep into the Town, would be too severe to even imagine. I would sometimes sprint into the invisible dog fence, and receive a nauseating shock, but my sister, Mirjana, never had so much as a wayward toe. *Nay rather!* she would say. *Rather I would try to squeeze water from bricks. Rather I would trap a bat in my own hair.* She just started to talk like that one day and it lasted for a couple of years, and although I loved her I could never decide whether to devote my strength to laughing at or choking her. [. . .]

CHAPTER 7

Our bodily changes began one midwinter when we were ten, a midwinter that stretched out intractably, bringing (we heard) despair to the Town, as the ground remained frozen. [. . .] One night, the Chancellor decided that he could coax forth the late spring. He crossed the invisible dog fence, whispering names we did not know were our own. The standard ritual used to whistle up spring called

Once, I was only interested in trying to see through people. Now nothing fills my heart like a person willing to stand up and look at me and block out the sun. Now I cannot imagine wanting to see anything beyond the breathing being before me, talking and gesturing and laughing, all for my sake.

for animal flesh, wine, and unwilling females, so he dumped out raw hamburger under our window. Then he lit a torch, peered inside, and immediately found our eyes. He was not meant to look at us like that. Then again, we were not meant to look back. But his gaze was proof of how human-like we'd become. [. . .]

always fumbling / always fretting / behind
on projects / behind on thank-yous / could
not follow / could not lead / could not talk
/ could not crawl / could not sweep properly / could not keep a secret / could not
dance well / could not chew well / did not
write as many letters / did not place as many
calls / did not stay awake long enough / did
not work hard enough / did not understand
quickly enough / did not wash enough / did
not cut short enough / ever misreading / ever
tripping / faked prayers / faked sleep / faked
listening / faked talent / faked competence /
faked health / going the wrong or inefficient
way / going back to fix because failed the
first time / had secretly stained / had been
unable to leave alone / had lied / had mis-
represented / had not trusted / had not been
brave / had not been faithful / had nothing
to climb up on / had nothing to fall off of /
invariably insincere / invariably contrived /
just about but not quite / just forgot the one
monolithic thing / kept his secret / kept in
contact / lacking the attention span / lacking
the ambition / lacking the empathy / made
excuses / marked absence with indolence /
marked every occasion with overindulgence

Often, I'd catch myself behaving stupidly in public. I'd have my head tilted in an idiotic way, my stomach sticking out. Or I'd try to be biting and witty, and stammer instead.

/ not enough food for the guests / no longer working / no longer as flexible / never not eaten by worry / never not eaten by distrust / opening the wrong door / offering the wrong type of comfort / prepared a bad meal / prepared stupidly and at length for an imaginary meeting / quiet when others needed chatter to soothe them / quiet in the face of another's agony / quiet in the presence of great cruelty / racing away from desire / racing away from fruitful temporary discomfort / said yes then didn't do it / said no and then did / taught the wrong lessons / undid the careful work of others / vicious responses to gentle corrections / vicious responses to gracious rejections / wanting protection wanting loyalty while offering it to nobody / X in the inappropriate boxes / yearning of the wrong type / yearning for the stupid the vain / zealous only in performative self-abasement / actually unable to forgive self or others / actually far more frightened than is feasible practical possible to admit

I had contended all of my life
With the urge to tunnel as far into the earth as possible
Thinking that, in this way, I could reach the sublime
(I wanted, more than anything, to exist without precedent)

Once I was not afraid to have strangers in my house,
Because the objects that could indict me would never be found
Once I had dreams that I told no one of
I dreamed of a row of disembodied male heads bobbing
I dreamed I collected four to six magazines and pulled down my pants
And positioned myself carefully over these male heads
And then shit in each of their mouths

Moreover, I dreamed that they had begged me to do this

And I dreamed that once I finished they cleaned me with their mouths
And then used those same mouths to make me come

Now I understand that nothing about me should appear whole
I understand that I must perform brokenness and vulnerability and need
Even if—
Especially if—
I feel none of those things

One morning I'm woken by a smell
Our cold medicine has simmered on the stove all night,

Cayenne, ginger, lemons, and honey, and I have slept poorly, I froze
around eleven—
The radiators failed
To brighten and hum,
And my cats deserted me
Now the bedroom like a dipped urn fills slowly with sunlight
As I swing my feet to the floor, and consider the state of my legs

CLOVER

She would pass through the fields swinging her arms, moving in clover and cyclamen, with her head thrown back and her whole body absorbing the gradual morning light, and then she would wake up somewhere near the electric fence, with the rain coming down, and her hair undone.

She lived miles outside of the Town, always with a dog to keep the property lawyers at bay. She called up each dog from the woods and they were all alike: one dog would die and another dog would jog seamlessly into his place. They all inhabited the same captive spirit.

Most terrible was the light in her head, chemically bright and lingering punitively on what she needed to forget. The shell that blew a hole in her leg, the years spent learning the Town's ugly language, the unhelpful neighbours, the constant suspicion. Instead, she forgot how to use her stove, she forgot which countries had bordered her own, she cleaned the bathtub with icing sugar instead of bleach.

Meanwhile, the lawyers, trying to steal the tiles out from under her feet. The dog circled the house endlessly. Labelled objects appeared in her vision, the letters neat and the details in perfect relief, clear as an infomercial, and then they vanished. She had unknowingly spent all of yesterday thinking a sentence, forgetting it, then thinking it again.

An animal that dies in the deepest part of the ocean
spends days falling miles to the bottom,
in view of all the living.

Once, buying groceries, she had drifted away and woken hours later in a wheelchair, her nails clipped like an infant's, a nurse trying to determine whom she belonged to.

Sometimes she imagines her body melting, too: her flesh running in a creamy stream over her slanting bedroom floor, and under the door.

I think about my mother's migration. Her green house emptied room by room, while she stood by and refused to submit. Even the whole of her belongings and savings was deemed inadequate by the Town's government.

One morning, the lawyers assemble muttering on her porch: *Freshwater pearls tucked in with her slips. Liquid stocks, an oil deposit on the south side of Town.* Some lawyers have bathed, drawn lipstick mouths. She laughs and shows them her palms.

Later, she wakes in the field at night, her face buried in her dog's side, his heartbeat unfindable. So many beings have passed into then out of her care.

After her brother's body washed ashore,
Roman spent time dogsitting in a house on
the west side of the Town. There was the
pressing matter of her own body and what to
do with it, so she fed it intermittently, walked
it like she walked the dog, and washed its
hands. The house was dominated by a spiral
staircase that she did not climb; in fact, she
eventually forgot the second floor existed.

Outside, the Town held a street fair. Women
rubbed raw chickens with paprika and locked
them in barbecue cages; people in latex
handed out smoothie samples. Down the
street, elderly men floated out of the nurs-
ing home like pressed flowers from a novel,
cotton balls scotch-taped to the insides
of their arms. Inside the house, Roman
made the plainest meals: recipes consisting
mostly of flour and water that she found
in a cookbook written by monks. She had
this cookbook; she had her mind's civilizing
impulse, which is to say, her resistance to
self-indulgent grief; she had the radiance of
her memories, and the terrific rate at which
they were fading. At night, the dog circled

her warily, but they were both too afraid to lie down.

One day a friend sent a doctor, and the doctor ran her gold-tipped fingers over Roman's body, pressing gently on her liver and lungs, lungs that (she was ashamed to admit) had newly begun to feel like they were filling with liquid. She despised her body for engineering this sympathetic reaction. It was like that time she had walked through the house and random objects (a blender, a space heater, a garlic press) appeared to emit light, as if she were underwater, and pushing through swaying weeds to find her brother. Roman found this delusion grandiose and narcissistic. But as the doctor peered into her ears, she allowed herself one memory.

Roman and her brother used to do something they called Famous Dancing, though of course they were not famous and it was not dancing: it was a kind of gymnastics routine performed to *Swan Lake*. Being older and stronger, Roman would lift and twirl her brother; they cartwheeled in unison, did back bends and splits. During the rare times they performed for their parents, to calm her nerves, Roman would retreat to the place that they were building together, every night before bed, in their shared mind. That uninhabited city they had designed, whispering back and forth between their bunk beds, with its defunct caramel factory and abandoned fairground and feral llama population: some llamas grave and funereal, some llamas with overbites.

Roman always fell asleep first, during these nights of construction. Much as she tried to stay awake, she always faltered in her purpose, though she never wanted to leave her brother building their city, its race tracks and strip clubs and burger shacks, out loud, alone in the dark.

Wait until you know that you only deserve whatever is free and right in front of you and not wanted by anyone else. I cried so much I stopped wearing makeup. What I remember most clearly—

Zeyna and I met when we were nine, and determined to make ourselves ugly in order to avoid the attentions of the Town's men. We had few ideas and no money and not much of an imagination between us. So we ate cigarette butts, we rubbed shit in our hair, we smashed our teeth with hammers— these were the more trifling behaviours. I will not tell you the rest.

Later, Zeyna spent months touring the Town doing a poorly received piece of performance art that involved humping the air and screaming while wearing a fluorescent skeleton suit and an upside-down cow mask. She still blames me for the damage she did to herself over those scant months when we were trying to take ownership of our flesh.

Today, we are flung out on her lawn like worms after rain, and I know that she hates me, a little; I know that she wishes I would die, a little, because I co-created the body she has now, and it is a body with much to hide. Zeyna is painting her bathroom and has taken down her checkerboard shower curtain; we are lying on it. I alone am sweating. She's wearing a moonstone ring—like her, it seems to aggressively resist being part of this world. In fact, both Zeyna and the ring look like objects retrieved from an ancient shipwreck, and I am jealous of her long, polished, hairless body in its gold lamé bikini and cannot, as a result, stop staring at it and tearing up handfuls of grass.

When I am around Zeyna, I worry constantly about hygiene. I shave my arms and legs before one of our appointments, as if I'm preparing to have sex with a stranger. I select enormous sun hats that leave most of my face in shadow. I choose loose dresses made of the thinnest silk; they hint at my body without fully admitting to its presence within them. These dresses cost more than a month in the hospital, and Zeyna is the only person who sees them. Some women, it seems, have a knack for cleanliness; she is one of them. She wanders over to her garden and eats a handful of nasturtiums. She seems to mostly live on flowers. On the windowsill she's brewing tea in a mason jar. I see lemon slices and feathery, celestial herbs.

Black squares, white squares, the spectacle of her body splayed over both. My body infecting the whole yard. *You have less soul than a dog*, I say to myself. *What?* says Zeyna. She can easily hide her damage with makeup and tattoos, whereas I work from home and can only swim at night or while wearing a wetsuit. If you met me you would find me too effusive, because I desire so much to be accepted. I know people think I'm revolting; I watch them duck into shops and slide down alleys—everyone retreats from my florid compliments, my wet eyes and close talking. If anything I own is admired, I feel compelled to give it away. I press upon bewildered strangers my earrings, my sandwiches, my shoes.

I'd like to be able to choose the work I do, the hours I keep. I would like the cleanliness that I achieve only through great difficulty to mean that I am no longer distracted by the question of my own cleanliness. But in trying to vanquish my body I have rendered it more visible. I am marked over and over again by my own attempts to vanish.

Zeyna is narrowing her eyes at me as she always does when she senses I am drifting. I want to tell her how hard it is to focus when I feel myself flowing over or shrinking from my clothing, protruding at odd angles, shivering then sweating. When I long to gather my stomach and my breasts into my hands and slice them cleanly off. If I were capable of gentleness I would want my breasts to just fall off, like raindrops. I'd like to rise, and leave my body sleeping on the rubber sheets it requires: entirely oblivious, and made beautiful by my absence. I'd like to dissolve into substancelessness, like a bouillon cube dropped into boiling water. These are the kinds of stupid desires I form my life around.

The Town that surrounds us fills with mist and the men in all of their despicable freedom saunter or skateboard right up against its borders. I want to ask Zeyna: how do you manage to seem happy to be alive? But she will not let me get close enough to her scars to lift the edges and peer inside. The long slices down her face healed with barely a trace; her boyfriend the Chancellor terrorizes her but he also funds many of her reconstructions. She will not speak of our time together. The more I see of her the more surely I know she has closed herself to me. One eye open, one eye shut, half in sun, half in shadow.

I knew he was a bad boyfriend but I didn't know how bad; none of us did. He was not a human being in the regular sense of those words. But I've never regretted one second of knowing him.

Hours later, so slowly, I walk to the river
From nowhere the wind
Floats the sound of bells toward me: circular, crystalline, impervious

I'm wearing my fluorescent orange hunter's hat
And the acid-proof boots the Chancellor insists upon
For he claims the water's full of mercury and fluoride
Like the hair and skin of an aging dentist

I round the last corner, I lift away
The single fir branch blocking my view
And I see a naked woman—one of the five Rachels—immersed
In the part of the river that pools, dammed by a fallen oak,
With shale steps rising on two sides

Her shoulders are slightly out of the water, and her breasts are floating
loosely
In a way that embarrasses me
She's leaned her head against the rock shelf as if in a hot tub,
And I'm close enough to make out the freckles across her shoulders
Her eyes have been shut for some time now

I remember those eyes covered by the Chancellor's hands
In the last gif he posted of this Rachel

She is naked
Her wounds are open
She is frantically sightlessly sanding a salad bowl

You're so revolutionary he exhales into her ear
The forest around them flickering like television

HAPPY MOTHER'S DAY!

My mother is the strongest woman I know

On this day of days

Mother's Day

I would like to pay tribute to her

My mother is

The most radiant woman in the world

I would like to simply say

Hello

Mom

Thank you for bringing me into this life

Thank you for *giving* me life

You were always there when I needed you

You were always a shoulder to cry on

Arms to hold me

Lips to kiss away my tears

My mom nurtured me when I was a child

Supported me when I was a young woman

Went through my sulky teenage phase

Right by my side and didn't bat an eye

Or raise a fuss

My mother is the strongest woman I know

My mother is the most

Beautiful woman I have ever seen

Inside and outside

My mother is the smartest kindest

strongest woman I have ever known

She has never given up on me even in my darkest hours

On this

The most special of holidays

Mother's Day

I would like to pay tribute to her

Even when her hands are covered in barbecue sauce or urine

I still want them to be reaching for me

Even when she is beyond resuscitation

   and her ribs have been broken by the paramedics

I want her to be thinking
                               Only of me

   My mother has an amazing track record

                               Of caring for others

Especially animals

       Which she loved

             Our Town had a pet shelter

She was a volunteer

You could barely manage to pry her hands off the kittens

My beautiful hardworking mother

                would have to be hustled out the door

She would almost always exit weeping

   Because that is just the kind of mother she was:

Everlasting

My mother is the most resilient woman in the galaxy

On this momentous occasion I would like to honour her

My mother rose every morning and met the world

with her true and naked face

And her long porny nails

My mother overcame the raw material of her life

and flourished

Intolerable to imagine

Her flight from this world

Today I would like to say

Thank you

Mother

For always standing by my side

For always having my best interests at heart

For always putting my needs

First

I remember this Town's early years. I remember most clearly the friendly ducks in the public garden. Now when I wake up I must battle the feeling of having been transplanted overnight to an enemy's house with no food or water or bedding and a centreless sun burning through the holes in the roof.

For always putting me

                    First

For always

                    Holding

My body in front of hers

                    Like a shield

FACTORY MEAT VII

Flood me with the light
Of the coldest eye in the heavens
Let the earth's coldest sea
Rush in and cover me

In this silence I attain
An absolute majesty
I feel a surge of power
Overwhelm me

I met Estelle Saltern in a park one morning, and though she was a stranger I intended to tell her everything about my life and how it had gone wrong. She was an old woman, this Estelle, and when I sat down beside her I first played with the frayed ends of her hair, and then I lay my head on the space where her breast once was.

She was famous for taking on the appearance of the most attractive thing around her, so soon she looked like the small pond: calm, silver and glinting. Indeed she looked so much like the pond, young children set tiny paper boats on her, and a few geese, confused, landed on her shoulders. While I talked about the father I'd hated, whose later-life care I'd neglected, Estelle Saltern slowly changed her appearance. For a few moments she resembled a newly opened orchid, but then, when a dark-haired young man entered the park, she took on his face and body for a time.

I told her my secrets as I would tell a trusted therapist and she said things like *You resilient thing! You brave thing! You conscientious thing!* in just the tone I craved. I wanted a reason to continue to exist, and Estelle Saltern seemed prepared to provide me with one. Her mouth when she said these things barely opened, and her hands were occupied with winding an infinite spool of blue thread.

I soon told her about the man who used to put his dick in me, until he deemed me too old. *I even* helped *him put his dick in me!* I cried, and such was Estelle's effect on me that I could immediately see the humour in my outcry. *It is the winter of your life*, she giggled, and I knew it was true. I was waiting for the Chancellor to sweep me off the earth.

Eventually, after I had spilled out most of my pathetic history, we said goodbye and she rolled slowly back across the park, this time resembling a wild strawberry that was part of a picnic being held by the fountain. Was there something to be learned from her alterations? I was not sure. I sat on the bench for a while, envying or dismissing other women's bodies as they walked past. Estelle Saltern and I were lucky to live in a town of such variety. Yet I wanted to tell her how it felt like there were only young people everywhere, strolling and smoking, and somehow, even if they were meek or slender, not leaving room for anyone else.

Did you not once find me beautiful? Did you not once find me rich? It is like I never existed.

Later, in my home, I shuddered and wept. I lay carefully on top of my quilt and touched my dirty face, my frizzy hair, my stiffening body, and I felt the familiar waves of shame and revulsion break over me. Could I rise? Could I join Estelle Saltern? And could she anoint me, and could we travel together in bodies that soon would be indistinguishable from the falling sun?

THE FUNERAL DIRECTOR VOICES
HIS OPINION

I had warned her that she might be inviting attack, that her physical presentation was not what it should be, that the Town did not welcome gaudy religious iconography, that she should not cover her face, her hair, that it was imprudent to flaunt her difference. For her funeral, I have wrapped her carefully in the patriotic linens of her town, which, of course, is not *this* Town. Her family, who could not afford to attend, sent a gift of unknowable flowers with spikes and hideous accusing faces. These I stored in the back of the funeral parlour, and later I crushed their heads and bent their stalks and stuffed them in the trash. I knew some of the facts of what she suffered, living here, but I could not recognize my own Town in her words. I simply could not recognize it.

I return to the property
I walk over the farm unfastening things
The gate from its hinges
The lock from the coop
I tug on my sweatshirt until it hangs to my knees
I vomit my ration of turmeric honey
I loosen the soil around the potato plants
I turn on the hose and let it spray uselessly into the dirt
I hear my own voice and it's calling me
A novice practitioner, full of mere pain I mistook for resolve—

But the dogs are alerted to something within me
They pour down the hill in a black wave toward me
Crowned by the foam of their own rabid frothing
Still I open every door in the Farmhouse I break every window
I run every tap and light every burner—

Things our former mayor liked: 1. Laws. 2. Butter. 3. Composting. 4. Fentanyl. 5. Kindness. 6. Her grandfather's suits. She had been a good and fair mayor; she was a creature of curious depth and strangeness and endless strength. She would lend her ear to anyone who needed it; she broke her back for her neighbours on moving day. She created laws that helped the old, the poor, the sick, and the vulnerable, unlike the Town doctor who had run from her responsibilities, unlike the Town mystic who had embarrassed us with her fervour. She had come to the Town from far away, from a place we derided as polluted and primitive, and she often remarked on how the air here was almost too fine and rich for her lungs. See: she was charmingly modest!

She had been told the truth of our Town's policy for mayors of her particular *background*: that they were allowed to rule, perfectly or imperfectly, for five years, and then they were broken down and brought to the burial cairn on the neighbouring island. She had agreed to these terms, but when her time comes we are disappointed to find her weeping in the barnyard amidst her scattered papers. A billowing red mist appears to be emerging from her heart. The goats are nibbling her bowed head. We place our hands upon her, we pick her up using all the gentleness at our disposal, and we pass her over our heads, toward the water. Had the moment been less solemn she would have realized the pleasures of crowd surfing. We move her toward the shore, where the strongest of us are waiting with the boat.

For the mayor's sake we had hoped for grey skies, but instead the day is driving its sunlight down our throats. We pile into the boat, and power it with eight people per side. Our mayor is laid out on the bottom. She is dressed in a suit and one of her mother's brooches—this one a small arrow piercing a ruby. We are not sure of the condition of her face; it is wrapped in a scarf. Her body has, by and large, maintained its integrity. The mayor makes no sounds.

Haltingly, we move in the water, splitting a path through the ice. The sea is a series of white, silver, and opal striations. The cold roots in our chests and blooms, spreading to the filaments of each lung. The dark fuzz of fir trees seems so far away. These are always

My last night on earth, I salt my bath, I coat my face in honey, I wash my hair with fragrant creamy chemicals. I open a beer, I light a cigarette, I shave one leg, I shave another.

the very worst moments, with our mayors. What can we say? What comfort can we offer? She will be remembered. But we cannot guarantee that she will be treated gently.

To exist at once in a state
Of absolute terror, and absolute agency

My fear of the Chancellor's death understood to be merely
My fear of the sublime

Whose dream is this
It is too sweet to be mine alone

With ease with hope with fear
With hatred with impatience
With extremity with urgency with rage I find him

OPEN HOUSE

This is the living room

I've always been a fan of the vaulted ceiling

We used linen and silk throughout

She used to curl up with a pillow and her morning espresso

I slept on the futon with a newspaper over my face

The floors were done with the intention of being easy to clean

And also stepped on frequently

You will note the Scotch thistle at the centre of each ceramic tile

And seconds later you will note the surrounding desolation

You know how some marriages go

One day it's daffodils and lint rollers

The next you come home and she's at the stove

There's a perfume hanging in the air

The shower's running and she's about to flip an omelet but
    instead

She turns to you

I'm a great believer in folk healing

So we had this sunroom added about nineteen years ago

I hope you don't mind listening to me go on

Isn't it funny

I have a lofty new age friend but I myself am not lofty

Though I recited Tennyson to her the first time we met

I was eleven she laughed at my back all lumpy with deerfly bites

It was summer and she worked on me like a crowbar

Though she was only nine

This is the bedroom my legs still ache when I look at the
    four-poster

Would you like to touch her raincoat would you like to wrap on
   her black dress

You think they wouldn't suit you

Well I guess you need a certain something to pull them off

I see you want me to get on with it

So this is the bay window here are the floorboards that is the
   ceiling

Let me pull the shades let me find the heat dial

I used to believe in the law of proximity

Oh don't nod like you understand

It's a term I made up

It is the belief that if you bear witness to something terrible

You will never directly experience

That terrible thing

Which does not explain why

At my age

And having lost her

I am finally being taken to the Farmhouse

We just passed the kitchen which was redone in I can't
    remember

Copper and a new fan, six burners

If you peer around that corner you'll see the bathroom and
    with any luck

No one will be in it

Clawfoot, skylight, keep it moving

No I'll need to pause here for a minute

I'll need you to go on without me

Can you hear that din

It's coming from the mountain to your left

She is passing overhead

I wake up in the morning on the floor of a furniture-less room. Everything removed while I dreamed. How did they manage to take the bed with me still sleeping in it?

Her span is exceptional

Even a town this big gets dark under the shadow of her wings

One summer in my youth the girl with Mercury tattooed
on her face ruled the Town, and I spent all my nights
wishing she would hitchhike to my parents' rotting house,
kick down the front door, and find me. Lying on top of my
comforter, I listened for the girl so hard I could hear the
tomatoes from our garden drying out in the oven. She
fucked all of her friends rotationally, catholically; she fucked
the grimy transients who slept rolled in plastic; she fisted
the Town councillor who had been fired for using too
many words in her speeches. The girl's mother had given
her a fanciful hippie name, and as a child she took a more
conventional one, but she could not remain an Amy for long.
Her attention could only be captured by the ugliest, most
violent, bravest, or most beautiful actions. And it was devas-
tating to watch her blast down the streets, embodying all the
inexpressible parts of myself.

I was so full of fear, I felt it from my toes to the ends of my
hair. Sometimes I was convinced that the fear had existed
before I did, for I was born to a legacy of poverty and filth.
In conducting even the mildest conversations with other
people, I felt like I was calling up for rescue from the
bottom of a well.

Every morning, I believed I could hear the comfortable
Townspeople rising from sleep and bending over to touch
their toes. I could hear their eggs poaching; I could hear the

rich, oily flavour being extracted from their coffee beans. And, in my youth, I measured their dignity against my family's degradation, for after my father left, the Chancellor paid for nurses to care for my mother, and these nurses were hostile and rough. My mother made distressed noises when they removed her shirt, and there were often food stains left on her face. Most days she was left propped up with pillows in front of a TV, vomiting as she was shown clip after clip of nauseating violence, for the nurses tuned to a livestream from the Farmhouse.

All my life, I craved nothing more than sex with a roomful of violent strangers. I wanted to be left with infections and polluted blood. I wanted to be left with a different face.

Watching this used to cause me such pain that I longed to find the girl, cast my body at her dirty feet, and beg her to lock me in armour. I'd look for her in the holiest part of the Town: the very edge, near the water, which was the source of disembodied, polyphonic singing. But the singing would always cease as I approached, and hours later I would wake cold and bruised in a field, with no memory.

I wanted to join the girl's army, if only she would let me. But she left after her sixteenth summer, while I stayed and conformed to the Town's punitive geography. Now, I imagine her being sewn into a wedding dress. I imagine her being sewn into a shroud. I imagine her being sewn onto my face. I try to capture the attention of others like her, though I know they will see me with perfect clarity, and find me laughable. Often, my life feels like a record of obsessions. I stand next to women on the bus and I hope a sudden brake will send them tumbling against me. When seated, I pretend to fall asleep so that I may slump onto the shoulder of the woman sitting beside me, only to wake immediately with a start, saying *oh pardon me I'm so sorry, I didn't know I was that tired.* And she responds kindly and absently, for I look friendly and middle-class, now, in my trench coat and dragonfly hairpin and mint-coloured nails; she doesn't yet see me for who I am, and I wonder, can I be reborn—

On this / The last morning I'd wake up / With
my original body / I put on all my plastic jewellery / I stood by the window / I ate a banana
covered in peanut butter / I bled through two
pairs of underwear and into my jeans / I tex-
ted six people / Begging each of them to fuck
me / While I still had / This body / When
I started to move / I passed many filthy /
Children alone / I received no texts back / I
was racing through the Town / I was trying
to incite / I was trying to provoke / The same
way I repeat / Over and over / The actions
that make me sick / That night / The night
in question / I biked past the seething pur-
ple water / I arrived at the botanical garden
/ Just as the nightwalkers left / Just as the
sprinklers turned on / Long after the plants
/ Had lowered their faces / And closed their
eyes / One man followed me / I thought: / He
is lonely / Two men followed me / I thought:
/ Pure coincidence / One man spoke / He said
/ *Why are you moving* / *At such* / *A leisurely* /
Pace / *It is too late* / *For such leisure* / *And you*
/ *Are too* / *Alone*

I have dug down into myself and found /
Nothing / I have lurched my way across this

Town to the water and found / Nothing / I
stopped eating / I stopped drinking / I wore
a steel breastplate / How quickly I became
intolerable / Even to myself / I was not permitted to have / The remains of the fetus
/ Scraped out of me / I was told to pass it /
Naturally / I will leave this old body behind /
I will reach the Oracle / I won't ask for proph-
ecy / I will ask to perform an exchange / My
old body for a new body / A new body pore-
less / Impermeable / Unetched / Unbranded
/ By even / The mark of its maker / I cannot
wait to die / Yes I know this will be / No real
death / From miles away still / The Oracle
says / *Keep moving* / *You have seen my face* /
Before / *It has made as little impression on you*
/ *As the face of the woman who makes your cof-*
fee / *The face of the woman you pay for maga-*
zines / *The face of the deaf woman* / *Who roams*
the library / *Asking you to buy* / *Her homemade*
greeting cards

I am panting / I am climbing / The mountain
on the outskirts of Town / The Oracle will
be found at its summit / My mouth is full of
my own dust / Lines from my own poems
/ Rise unbidden in my mind / Humiliating
me / Making me laugh too / Neon roadside
flowers / Tiny stars of chamomile / Moving
faster now / Rocks in my sandals / Dirt on

my contact lenses / Circled by deer flies / Thus far unbitten / The hate I harbour / In my limbs / My organs / The hate I harbour / In my eyes / My mouth / The hope of women / Is murder / One man is following me / Could be coincidence / Two men are following me / Oink Oink / They say / Wind coming over / Rain coming down / Day of radiance / Beep Beep! / Says a tourist in a white duck hat / Moving past me / I recall / The food processor at my restaurant job / Feeding peeled carrots into it / Whole / And finally / When I pass a woman vomiting on the trail / I do not wait for the other pilgrims / To recognize her as the Oracle / And plant a thicket of crutches around her / I pause and cup her bald and tattooed skull / I brush the pollen from her shoulders / I pick a caterpillar off her neck / I scatter the coins of my eyes at her feet

Don't be afraid don't be afraid don't be afraid. There there there there there. This is it.

FACTORY MEAT X

I enter his body

I unscrew all its valves and let in the sea

His face, from up close, is pitted and rippled like the surface of the moon

His rolled-back eyes, my memory of their wretched unfathomable blue

My grandfather spent afternoons in the woodshed drinking rum and speculating about my dead mother's provenance. He'd wheel over the dirt floor covered in sawdust, barking.

He hated my mother's skin, the shape of her eyes, characteristics I have inherited. *Where'd you get those fuckin eyes.* I felt I had retrieved them in the most despicable way—as if, with scooped-out sockets, I had plunged a toilet only to find that my eyes were the objects clogging it.

I would arrive before my grandfather in the morning and he would pull me onto his lap and perform exercises intended to test the speed of my breathing and the responsiveness of my muscles. Then he would scrape my hair into a ponytail, perfume me with rosewater, and send me to the stove to shake cinnamon over his oatmeal.

In moments of rage he would call me close to his face. *You are a bowl of fruit,* he would say. *Which fruit should I remove from you first?*

I despised him. Despite this, his anger emptied my heart.

My heart. Deboned, scraped and salted, packed away so tight in my chest.

Eventually forked out of its cavity, passed through spruce smoke, and set on fire.

+

Hello. In the dream of my life I'm rich, reckless, and furred, gleefully unpleasant, and shining with all the metals I attract.

But, as a teenager, I was removed from my grandfather's care and brought to the Farmhouse to be kept by the Chancellor. I hated myself. More than that: I disgusted myself. My craven, predictable addiction to suffering, my longing for punishment, my desire to be forced.

And the Chancellor beheld these secret afflictions.

And he cupped his hands as my body poured forth, like chaff from a threshing machine.

+

What was my life then?

What was my life then besides fortunate?

Bolted to my throne, sacred and specialized, and approached as one might approach a holy relic: Lo it is I, the beloved skull or finger.

After the first decade, memories began to surface in my mind. One summer I was swimming in the ocean and saw an approaching wave on which inexplicably floated thousands of dead blackflies. That is how I used to feel watching my grandfather advance in his wheelchair toward me.

+

In my middle years, the Chancellor and I would walk together the long path to the marigolds that fringed his property. As his body warmed from his efforts, duelling perfumes arose from it.

I did not yet understand the immensity of the poisons I had ingested.

+

At the end of my youth, ravaged by cancer, I was finally permitted to travel.

The pain was untenable. I bargained with it, I told the pain who I would kill, who I would betray, the hopes I'd abandon and the sex I'd decline, if only it would stop.

For months, I was ferried to hospitals throughout the Town, where diseased parts of my body were sliced off, pickled, then divided into ever-daintier portions.

My doctor's delight in these verbs: sliced, pickled, divided; once she told me my leg wound might *fillet* open; how I wanted to marry her, her and her golden nails, then, as in now; someday, meaning immediately.

I felt like a neighbourhood barbecue of varying cancerous meats, a picnic table studded with rotten sweetbreads. I invite you to set a dish of mustard beside my sticky, caramelized leg.

+

Thereafter, what was my life?

Rescued/abandoned/cherished/forlorn, all these grievous gaps in my theories, my history.

For my convalescence, I was returned to the Farmhouse, but I was too old to heal into a fuckable shell.

All day, while the Chancellor pondered my fate, I swung in my hammock above him, dripping infrequently onto the sloping stone floor.

All day he sat at the table, writing minutely on graph paper, shining with sweat even under the programmed fans, trembling with pleasure each time he allowed himself to eat.

His hand would shake so he could barely bring food to his mouth.

+

Most perfect reminders of substancelessness: my tended wounds, each morning's pour of light, the ocean's milky turquoise water inching daily closer to our door, and beholding the Chancellor, as the stick beholds the flower.

+

Was I always bound?

Was I always bound to come to this?

Helpless, caged, and dripping.

Devoted to cultivating my shame and abjection.

At night, the obsequious moon cast light on the glittering gems in the Chancellor's teeth.

+

I listened to the bones move around in my body.

I remembered myself as a child, obsessively attuned to the needs of my grandfather.

We had a dynamic; it went like this. I would say *Who do you want me to be?* And then he would tell me, and then I'd become.

+

How long will I last? I asked.

The Chancellor took a long time to answer. Meanwhile, he rubbed into his enormous white hands a softening cream the scent and texture of toothpaste.

+

Relentless sawing away at form.

+

When I placed my ear to my thigh I could hear my blood rushing to foam. My braid hung down like a wet snake, and I no longer allowed my wounds to be washed.

I was reaching some uncharted place within me, and every day the Chancellor watched me plunge deeper, but he was helpless to stop me.

I could tell when my gaze—ever-weakening though it was—began to frighten him.

+

There are so many ways to hold a human prisoner.

I am now only held prisoner by my chosen devotion.

I have discovered the spectacular release of finally inhabiting flesh that precisely embodies my self-conception.

A kind of teenage dream, this perfect match between interior and exterior.

I want to describe for you the tremendous satisfaction of this feeling.

But the phrases that come to mind are all so sexual and embarrassing.

+

The Chancellor recognizes this new certainty in me.

You've always been so morbid, he says, pretending to stretch and yawn, but I see something shift in his eyes.

+

Eventually, I could see directly into my own soul.

I had always visualized a layer of black gunk at the bottom of it.

But that layer was absent.

The architecture of my soul was not remotely what I had imagined.

The air was warm and vaporous, the ground was clear and greening, and the sourceless light was softer than any I'd seen.

That day, I knew I could do it. I felt as certain of my own ability as I felt of the position of my heart within my body.

I found my teeth, and I tore a hole.

I rose above my fallen form like steam.

I released the cheerful and reckless devil within me.

Keep your speeches short! I hissed at the Chancellor.

May the earth bless you and put you to use, I said to my body, and that was the end of my voice.

It was early morning, and over the hill near the water I heard a few faint coughs, then the singing began, and that was the end of my hearing.

There was no light, but neither was there a pursuer, and that was the end of my vision.

+

Follow water. Block the sun.

I cannot see what waves are at my feet.

I cannot feel what winds are at my face.

+

Now there is the sensation of plunging.

Now there is the sensation of falling.

Now I will sleep in a rush of bubbles.

+

What if I had a secret?

What kind of secret?

The kind that would devastate you.

+

Whose hands are these. Whose arms. Whose voice.

Whose voice, flashing over the black waters.

It is here for only a moment and then it is gone.

+

Infinite night, moonless and steady.

Drift in a veil of white noise.

+

Don't ever leave me.

I'll never leave you.

+

Arrival upon this new shore, water running swift and deeply green, like a sudden rush of spring.

The sand frozen in waves, and littered with shipping containers.

Rusted, anonymous, studded with barnacles, they are not only mine, they are everywhere.

For so long, I wanted from him the impossible. Utter autonomy, and utter abjection. I wanted him to feel the totalizing force of my love, and the totalizing force of my hatred, all at the same time.

+

In each, by damage or design, there is some form of entry.

A door, a window, a crack, a hole.

Rhoda went to bed certain that she would get the call in the morning, and so her nighttime preparations were both entirely normal, and tinged with an otherworldly and melancholy anticipation. She turned on the TV, she ate a dinner of banana muffins broken apart in a bowl and covered with pink sugar-free yogurt, remembering how she and her roommate ate the same meal for a week years ago, watching the ice storm pass over their heads.

Her roommate, Lee, had been very good with privacy. She had never entered Rhoda's room, and Rhoda had never entered hers. They had been roommates for sixty years. Neither had ever married; both had escaped the Chancellor's notice. Lee had bought her a refrigerator magnet in the '80s that said "I'm a great housekeeper. I just sweep the room with a glance." Two weeks ago, Lee had fallen and broken her hip. While in the hospital, she finally admitted the new heaviness of her head. And now she was dying, or rather, now other people knew she was dying, with a tumour on her brain so large that her eyes were being slowly forced from their sockets. Soon the apartment would fill with flowers. And there was this feeling (which Rhoda had had all day) of being scrutinized, somehow, as if in these last moments of Lee's life, she must do her best to be as groomed and composed as possible.

So Rhoda had showered and set her hair and made certain to eat with a straight back. She did not touch her face. Once she swore at a game show host but then she quickly apologized. She felt so convinced of spectral presences that she was embarrassed when she noticed that she had not fully rubbed in her night cream and her cheeks were streaked white. She spent ten minutes facing the sink before turning on the tap. When she lay down in bed she did so in a way and at an angle that she thought could only be evaluated as modest. Rhoda had always had the smaller room, the result of an unspoken pact. Her bed was as narrow as a nun's or prisoner's: perhaps two feet wide and five and a half feet long.

I would be happy to see you, or anyone. I will accept visitors at any time of the day, or the night. I step in the shower, and I sit down.

The china in her cabinet rattled once when the upstairs neighbour's washing machine got stuck in the spin cycle. When the radio spoke briefly of sex, she fell asleep. A noiseless wind pressed against her door.

For weeks, the radio has been talking about the drought that will soon hit the Town. And when Rhoda wakes up she feels that she has barged in on some imaginary concerned citizen's forum being held by her bedroom furniture. Every object seems to offer silent rebuke. Her bureau appears more fully driven into the corner, as if it too were retreating from her. Rhoda reflects on her own use of water, on washing Lee's shoulders and back. She knows when Lee's birthday is, but not how old she is turning.

Rhoda knows the Town was formed on top of a vast, untouchable underground lake. Many Townspeople had died trying to reach that lake: their antennas would pick up the hiss and rush of the fresh, mineral-rich water tumbling over and over on itself, observed by no one and beholden to no pattern of being. As a child, she dreamed of finally reaching it, of pushing through a burst of white static into the suspension, into a new form of light falling like liquid swords on her face. Now, nothing brings Rhoda more comfort than knowing that no one will ever reach that world, the deep and secret heart of that lake, ungathered, unseen, all that water running miles below.

He was a brother / father / husband / boyfriend / cousin / grandfather / uncle / son. An employee / employer / acquaintance / boss / server / professor / janitor / researcher / coach. Friend / enemy / envied / scorned. Writer / thief / therapist / dermatologist / artist / musician / funeral director / architect. Activist / customer service agent / nightwatchman / grave tender / construction worker / priest / designer / surveyor / prep cook / teller / conductor / baker. A slacker / a bookworm / an A-type / a dreamer. Sober, a user, homeless, a homeowner. Kind and forgiving and tongue-tied and cruel and empathetic and well-spoken and fussy and laid-back and vengeful and sporty and outgoing and introverted and particular and neurotic and shy and violent and slobbish and clean and confident and wealthy and poor and educated and furious and gentle. He believed he resembled no one else on earth.

MY DARRYL DOESN'T LIKE TO EAT VEGETABLES one aunt, Jutta, said sternly to the other, Jude, and thus their estrangement began. They hated each other with perfect savagery, and so they presented each other with lavish gifts.

First, Jude gave Jutta an enormous book of photographs of water: the ideal gift for the one you hate most. Ponderous, abstract, impossible to argue with, weighing more than she did. Jude dropped it triumphantly on her sister's lap with a shout, nearly breaking her legs.

Next, Jutta gave Jude a pair of seamless fluorescent-pink suede boots that reached nearly to her pelvis and could neither be walked in nor exposed to the air. Later, Jude presented Jutta with an eighteenth-century embossed tin containing a written record of Jude's physical measurements, of which Jutta had always been jealous. Jutta's eyes widened then darkened as she unfurled the tiny scroll.

Five years into their dubious project, the aunts are exhausted and sorrowing. A repentant Jutta gives Jude the story of their lives together, from infancy to adulthood, built out of marzipan and mounted on top of an enormous buttercream cake. There are detailed marzipan figures to represent each of the important people in Jude's life. There are tiny reproductions of Jude's happiest memories, such as the time she rejected a marriage proposal. There is even a reproduction of the rented beach house in which the aunts had stayed at the end of their last estrangement. (They had once not spoken for two years, for reasons they'd both secretly forgotten.) They lived for a month in that beach house, and when one needed to escape the other's company, she would shower outside in the cedar enclosure, feign cramps, or take hours to dust a single room.

I'd hoped to make contacts; I'd hoped to move forward without her. I wanted him to like me. I always praised his work, but he never mentioned mine.

Otherwise, the aunts had filled the days with stunts. There was a marzipan replica of the afternoon they had climbed a power plant, and the night they had built a fire and fed it their phone bills and credit reports. But the marzipan scene that brought the aunts to reconciliation was built in the centre of the cake.

It was a near-flawless reconstruction of the next day, after the fire, when the aunts had felt rejuvenated and swum together in the orchard, in a giant trough that had been used for watering cattle. Black rubber and ugly, the rim of the trough was crusted with a delicate white filigree of dried cow saliva; it had never been properly cleaned. But for some reason it felt better than a river, lake, or ocean; the dark material absorbing the warmth of the sun, the water itself smelling faintly like licorice, the two sisters looking up at the apple trees over their heads, as fruit dropped occasionally into the water, and they murmured lazily to each other about the seafood restaurant they would open someday. Jointly they would buy up a swath of the coast. There would be roasted parsnip soup and there would be lobsters worked into nearly every dish. One aunt was in favour of driving scissors into each lobster's neck to kill it before it was dropped into boiling water, the other aunt was not. It didn't matter. Neither process would change the character of the meat.

When the school burned, our ghosts were released. For years, we'd only seen well-meaning psychics who entered the classroom to light candles and lay cards, while our ghosts looked on in embarrassed pity.

Once, long ago, we were human and frightened. When the gunman ordered all the males to leave the room, we crouched behind desks and tables with wet wheeling eyes, before being caught up by our hair and shot through our throats. Now, years later, we still had bodies, but our skins were loosening, our bones were emulsifying, our organs were growing cold within us, we were moving toward the third state.

There were fourteen of us and we travelled together, after the engineering school was torched, spooning at night and wringing out each other's hair in a comical manner, for we were conscious of our public, though we didn't have much of one. (We were followed by a melancholy choir of spectral admirers, but we learned to ignore them.) We mainly feared discovery by ghost hunters, historians, or other sweet-natured sentimentalists. This new life had the soft edges and sharp turns of a dream; indolent and luxurious, we roamed the outskirts of the Town at will. We moved with such silent assurance that walking through fields we would nearly step on wild animals.

We remembered being so hysterically naive, we thought we had no right to deny any part of our bodies to anyone. But after a month of this life, we no longer imagined vengeance against the gunman who'd stomped these old selves out of us. We no longer felt tethered to human vanities: we played host to all manner of insects and parasites. Being female, we had been taught to wonder when we would break off into factions and assemble against each other. We waited for the lies and betrayals to begin, and when they did not we knew that, in this way, we had defeated the gunman.

Soon we would pass into the third state, but for now, every morning we woke to gentler sun on our eyelids, and clearer air in our lungs, and we learned to speak of our own souls with great candour, so close did we feel to them, when before they had seemed like trick staircases to nowhere sealed behind glass.

As our flesh moved toward greater and greater transparency, you could find us holding up our hands to the light of the fires we built at night, to see our souls stirring gently under our skin, while miles away, we imagined, lightning moved over the open sea.

Black night, black stumps forked and trembling, but spring was forever. After each evening's rain, trees along the river sprayed in the wind for hours. I cannot believe another world exists.

Afterwards, great quiet

Faltering fires

Water coming up through the floorboards

A scatter of orange shells

Wind through the broken windows

Squirrels in the kitchen

(The gradual emergence

Of all our voices)

Red summer

Warm autumn

Bright winter

Black spring

EPILOGUE

REVA: We are long dead—

MIRJANA:—and the Town has mostly tumbled into the sea, when one October night we hear a racket in our necrotized cells.

REVA: We brush off the grave dirt, untie our death masks, and storm the murdered Chancellor's stinking and long-abandoned Farmhouse, Mirjana, Harriet, and me, three friends resurrected after years in our coffins.

MIRJANA: Slow down, how does it look?

REVA: The ground ripples.

MIRJANA: My manicured hand emerges from the dirt.

REVA: The grave tender sees us then averts his eyes— content to sit and smoke and eat his plate of meat and grapes.

MIRJANA: Now when we move we're attended by swirls of glittering phosphorescence.

HARRIET: WE ARE CITIES SEEN FROM A DISTANCE AT NIGHT!

REVA: In loose plastic shorts and studded T-shirts, synthesizers bolting out of Harriet's giant headphones, headphones she was buried in, headphones which she will not remove, even under duress.

MIRJANA: As if newly in love we are moved beyond measure by everything around us—the river passing close with its cargo of listening ears, the garden's rows of slimy kale and rotten lettuces. How the wind at our approach retreats, and tangles itself in the tree we used to climb.

REVA: We hold and release hands, we look into each other's eyes and then retreat from that looking.

MIRJANA: Tiny clicks and whirrs in the sky as morning arrives, the stars cascading geometrically, a shower of crystals.

REVA: The moon dangles mutely, eager to vanish.

HARRIET: I CARRY WITHIN ME A NAMELESS SORROW THAT I CANNOT EXPEL!

I FEAR TOTAL AND OBLITERATING LOSS!

I FEAR MERELY EXISTING IN A SUSPENDED STATE BETWEEN SPIRIT AND FLESH!

I AM FILLED WITH CORROSIVE AND INTRACTABLE SHAME!

I FEAR THE INTOLERABLE ACCUMULATION OF
YEARS OF THWARTED—

REVA and MIRJANA: SHUT UP WE FUCKING
KNOWWWWWW!

MIRJANA: There are two qualities Harriet lacks, vanity and
malice, and so forgiving her is easy.

REVA: Let's back up, let's disassemble, let's tell this story
differently.

MIRJANA: We were so young when we arrived at the
Farmhouse.

REVA: Teenagers. I was so filled with wonder.

MIRJANA: I thought I was so dumb.

REVA: I wanted to be endlessly admired and desired, and
also entirely hidden and safe.

MIRJANA: Those days of pregnancies and factory meat and
near-constant sleep, carefully sponged clean with dish
soap each morning by the Chancellor.

REVA: Like most teenagers, we were in search of the
highest note, the most perfect vibration, we wanted our
lives to feel like fables without *being* fables, exactly—

HARRIET: WHAT DOES THAT MEAN!

MIRJANA: My desire to cast myself out of my own body, my desire to inhabit another body, or not only another body, another spirit, whole, an inhabitation deeper than flesh—

HARRIET: ASSIMILATE! MODIFY! RENDER! MAKE OF ME SOMETHING GREATER AND FIRMER AND MORE OPEN, STRONGER AND MORE FIBROUS, ANTIQUE YET RESTLESS!

KNOWING US NOW, IN THESE GHOST FORMS, WITH ALL OUR FORCE AND CERTAINTY AND POWER, YOU CANNOT IMAGINE US BEING COERCED, BEING MANIPULATED, BUT THERE WAS A TIME—

REVA: I remember how I left—what I stole from the Chancellor, for I still believed it was possible to steal what was mine—pregnant, I crept from the Farmhouse one night, leaving you both behind, and I moved through the odourless garden and down the dirt road, until I was caught at the Town's border, and ruined. And the banality of my pregnancy-dreams was replaced by the banality of my grave-dreams: rain falling irregularly, a telephone ringing then not, a door that wouldn't stop slamming, a house with thousands of secret rooms. My body a haunted ruin.

MIRJANA: *Every* body is a haunted ruin!

HARRIET: MIRJANA CANNOT BEAR SELF-
SPECIALIZATION OF ANY KIND!

REVA: Moving on. Entering the Farmhouse, we note:

MIRJANA: In the kitchen, a wooden table cut with deep
lines, a fridge full of chicken livers, split bags of flour
thickened with glittering grey moth wings. The remains of
a few wooden salad bowls. A few dog skeletons.

HARRIET: A BURIED YET INDISPUTABLE POWER!

MIRJANA: In the living room: conscious terror.

REVA: Ambitionless wind.

MIRJANA: Our story told backwards, and wrong.

REVA: The ghost of the murdered Chancellor propped up
on his throne of meat.

REVA: In the washroom . . . oh. Okay.

MIRJANA: In the washroom, Harriet is drawing a bath, her
long hair wrapping around the faucet. The clean bubbles
are scented with cedar, the water is gaspingly hot as
always, for scar tissue is so much less sensitive than original flesh. Harriet is, of course, a mystic, a visionary, but
she has never seen herself as such.

HARRIET: I CAN'T EVEN ENVISION MYSELF
MAKING IT OUT OF THIS BATH!

MIRJANA: Now bats fly in and land on Harriet's arms. A
daddy-long-legs, timid handful of needles, is moving over
the white porcelain—now it's dipping an arm or leg in to
test her bathwater—like most other creatures, it's obvious
that it just wants to be close to her. She washes her matted
hair with vanilla-orchid slime.

REVA: I am leaving. I am entering the mud room.

(*pause*)

REVA: In the mud room, there is only me.

(*pause*)

REVA: I am standing here alone with my exceptionally, my
deeply and deathly, tired eyes.

+

(*Time passes*)

+

REVA: That first night I got very drunk and then very
hungry and fell asleep on a pile of fancy potato chips: red
curry, fish sauce, honey mustard.

HARRIET: I TOLD YOU!

MIRJANA: We burned a tray of cookies.

REVA: We twirled Mirjana into a ballgown.

MIRJANA: We said *slaughterhouse* into a mirror, and waited.

HARRIET: HA!

REVA: Later, Harriet and I walked the abandoned garden: spinach, dog shit, pepperoni, bones, and Harriet's practicality making her wonder what was edible.

+

MIRJANA: To create the séance—

REVA:—To reach our past selves—

MIRJANA:—first we clean the Farmhouse with pressure hoses, then we close all the doors, lock all the windows, and sponge-paint the ceiling silver. We want a sealed, hermetic feeling, like what the atmosphere pressure might be, were we encased in a Fabergé egg.

REVA: There must not be even a mouthful of fresh air in the house. We burn a choking quantity of incense. It infuses our hair and skin.

MIRJANA: Using my patented intricate stacking method, I built a fire guaranteed to burn for hours.

REVA: The fire is preening and beautiful and clearly delighted with her. It sends long, appreciative tongues of flame in Mirjana's direction for hours, reaching through the iron grate. Very hot; very sexual.

MIRJANA: Shut up.

(*Enter Harriet*)

HARRIET: I HAVE EMERGED FROM YET ANOTHER BATH WEARING THE PLUNDERED GOLD OF THE TOWN'S CONQUERED DYNASTY!

REVA: The turtle that vanished forty years ago to live under the bookcase watches the proceedings. We can't see him but if we could we would cry for his soft and wrinkled body, his loose skin, his eyes focused in their desire to see us with clarity, in all of our ludicrous details.

MIRJANA: The point is to return to who and what we were, before we were brought here. We will—

HARRIET:—ATTEMPT TO SYSTEMATICALLY REWIND OUR LIVES TO FIND THE UNTOUCHED, ORIGINAL SELF, THE DISAVOWED CORE, THE SELF WE HAD BEFORE THE SHAME TOOK ROOT, BEFORE THE TOWN BECAME OUR SOULS' CRUCIBLE, BEFORE

WE WERE BROUGHT TO THE FARMHOUSE,
BEFORE OUR BODIES WERE PROCESSED TO—

REVA AND MIRJANA: WORDY!

REVA: We sit in a circle. I wind my braid around my head—

MIRJANA: I catch my tears before they fall—

HARRIET: I LEVITATE BRIEFLY!

REVA: There is a temporary darkening of the silver-
sectioned sky—

MIRJANA: A shower of white-blossomed branches whips
the window—

REVA: And we all undergo a realization of the heaviness
and severity of the sudden rain.

MIRJANA: I turn to you—

HARRIET: I TURN TO YOU!

REVA:—I turn to you and your green eyes are barely iced-
over ponds, we can see the fronds moving separately
within them, and then, extremely deep down, we can see
your former self, floating belly up, serene and unfrozen,
merely asleep—

MIRJANA: Let us fold our hands, let us open our mouths,
just wide enough to speak—

+

The voice when it comes doesn't have quite the texture we
expected, the voice when it comes is like any of our voices, but
higher—it sounds slightly bored, but we must shed our expec-
tations and accept it—

+

Sit up straight, close your eyes—

No talking! No laughing! No texting!

+

We sought

We carried through agony

We renounced with force

+

In the newly artificial light we are one by one anointed

Made radiant and deathless

+

Faceless

Bodiless

Our fugitive selves emerge

+

So much awaits us

A tilted earth, a reddening sun

There is nowhere we cannot go

There is nothing we cannot become

FACTORY MEAT XIII

Rise, and greet your terrible
New being

I picture slowly entering a sea.

I step into the water dragging something behind me;
I have no idea what.

I have no idea what I'm dragging behind me.

NOTES

In "A Chorus of Ghosts," the phrase "I can't stand myself when you touch me" is borrowed from James Brown and his record of the same name.

"The Stages of Harriet" is conceptually indebted to Anne-Marie Turza's poem "The Glass Case."

"Teacher" was inspired by Pasha Malla's translation of Agota Kristof's short story "The Teachers," published in the fall 2017 issue of *The New Quarterly*.

"I Know You Are You, and Real" is a phrase from Jean Valentine's poem "X."

"Liquid Swords" is a title borrowed from GZA, a.k.a The Genius.

In "Factory Meat VI," the phrase "You're so revolutionary" is taken from Ryan Trecartin's 2004 video *A Family Finds Entertainment*.

"I Am Without Money, Pity, or Time" is dedicated with deepest love and gratitude to M. T. And, within it, the phrase "I cannot see what waves are at my feet" is intended to echo John Keats's "I cannot see what flowers are at my feet."

In "Slumber Party /// Spectral Trace," Harriet's line "I CARRY WITHIN ME A NAMELESS SORROW THAT I CANNOT EXPEL!" is indebted to a line by Emily Berry, "I carry inside me the trace of a threat that I cannot discharge," from her poem "The End."

"Rise, and greet your terrible / New being" is intended to recall the lines "O lullaby, with your daughter, and the innocence / Of your cold feet, greet a terrible new being" from "The Poem's Gift" by Stéphane Mallarmé, translated by A. S. Kline.

ACKNOWLEDGEMENTS

Nothing would be possible for me without the love and support of my friends, and my family—especially my mother, and my sisters.

All my love to Anastasia Jones, who is brilliant and fastidious, and who read—and improved—this book, so many times.

To Jessica Mensch, whose painting is on the cover: I am thrilled by you, and your amazing work.

To my agent, Martha Webb, who is both subtle and formidable.

To my peerless editor, Martha Kanya-Forstner. Her immersive empathy, delicacy, discernment, and vision.

Kristin Cochrane, thank you for your kindness, your humour, your support, and your advocacy.

I am very grateful to Jordan Ginsberg for his consistent and incredibly heartening encouragement. And to everyone at Strange Light: I am so honoured to be a part of your list.

Erin Kelly, Kimberlee Hesas, and Kaitlin Smith: thank you so much for your hard work and deep care. Jennifer Griffiths, thank you for your beautiful, innovative designs, inside and out. And to Shaun Oakey, who copyedited this book, and Melanie Little, who proofread it, thank you for your meticulous attention.

To the editors of the magazines and journals in which some parts of this book first appeared: thank you so much.

The Toronto Arts Council, the Ontario Arts Council, and the Canada Council for the Arts all supported the writing of this book, and I am immensely grateful. Thank you.

For everyone at Sistering: participants, staff, and volunteers. Thank you. I am so fortunate to be a part of your community. (From their website: "Sistering is a multi-service agency for at-risk, socially isolated women in Toronto who are homeless or precariously housed.") Donate here:

www.sistering.org

+

For J, to whom this book is dedicated. I love you.